The Pied Piper of Hamelin

Penny Dolan and Martin Impey

W
FRANKLIN WATTS
LONDON•SYDNEY

YOUNG PEOPLES LIBRARY SERVICES

County Council

Libraries, books and more...........

3/16

1 7 JUN 2017		
2 9 JAN 2018	2 1 DEC 2016	
? 1 ⌐? ¹?⌐8		
2 1 APR 2018		0 5 DEC 2023

Please return/renew this item by the last date shown.
Library items may also be renewed by phone on
030 33 33 1234 (24hours) or via our website

www.cumbria.gov.uk/libraries

Cumbria Libraries

CLIC
Interactive Catalogue

Ask for a CLIC password

1
A Fine Town

Many years ago, there was a town called Hamelin where the people had plenty of everything. The shops were fine, food filled every table and life was good – until a few rats arrived.

Before long, huge families of rats were running around everywhere, bold as brass. They took the meat and cheese from the cellars. They drank soup from the cook's pans and stole food from the plates on the tables.

They made nests in hats and chewed up shoes and clothing. Sometimes, the rats were squeaking so loudly that people could not hear themselves speak. Even at bedtime, there was no rest. The sheets were already full of rats.

The creatures were not afraid of anything.
They fought the dogs, chased the cats and
even bit the babies in their cradles. Soon,
the people had had enough.

2
The Plague of Rats

Angrily, the townsfolk marched to the
Mayor's chambers.

"Do something!" they shouted. "Our taxes
pay for your feasts and furs and finery,
Lord Mayor. Get rid of this plague of rats,
or go yourself!"

"Of course," the Mayor told them. "Don't
worry. Go home. Just let me think."

The Mayor called all his rich friends
together. They had no idea how to get rid
of the rats. "We will offer a reward for
someone who does," said the Mayor, and
they all agreed. The Mayor nailed the poster
up outside the Town Hall.

The very next morning, the Mayor and his friends heard a knock on the door.
"Enter!" called the Mayor.
In stepped a tall, thin man with twinkling eyes and a face full of smiles.
He wore the strangest old-fashioned garments and a flute was hanging at his shoulder.

"Your honour," he said, "I am the Pied Piper. I have cleared castles and palaces of pests and plagues in far-off lands. If you give me a thousand golden coins, I will rid your town of rats."

9

Everyone gasped.

"Do not worry. I have a plan," whispered the Mayor to his deputy. Then he turned to the Pied Piper and smiled. "A thousand?" the Mayor declared grandly, waving his hand in the air. "Rid us of these wretched rats and I promise you'll have fifty thousand golden coins. You have my word."

The Pied Piper nodded, bowed to the Mayor
and stepped out into the street.

3
The Pied Piper's Song

The Pied Piper's eyes twinkled. He lifted his flute to his lips and blew three long, soft notes. Within moments, hundreds of rats appeared, answering his call.

Off went the Pied Piper, all the way through the town. Rats appeared from everywhere as if the music would lead them to a place where there was all a rat could want. Squeaking and scampering, the plague of rats followed the Piper, running faster and faster towards their dream.

The Pied Piper reached the banks of the
great river. Although he stopped walking,
he did not stop playing and the rats did not
stop running. They streamed down the bank
and dived into that deep, cold river.

In moments, every single rat was gone.
The terrible plague was over. The people
of the town were so happy. They cheered
and rang all the bells.

Soon, the Pied Piper arrived back at the Town Hall, ready to collect his reward. The Mayor grinned, because he had a clever plan.

"Well done, Piper!" he said. "I hear the rats are well and truly gone."

"As I promised," replied the Pied Piper.

The Mayor shrugged. "But if there are no rats in the town, we have no reason to pay you, do we?" The Mayor threw some small coins at the Piper.

"Take these, you stupid fool, and be glad of what you get!"

The Piper's eyes blazed with rage. "No, Lord Mayor! It is you who are the fool,"
he declared, "and you and your
little town will be sorry that your promise
was broken."

4
The Piper's Revenge

The Pied Piper stepped into the street. Lifting his flute to his lips, he again blew three long notes. As he set off, striding through the town, children appeared in every door and alleyway and started running after him. Brothers and sisters 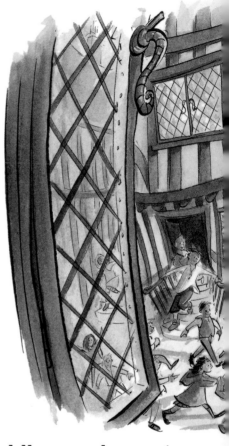 hurried along, bringing toddlers and carrying babies and more joined at each street corner. Soon every child in town was following the Piper's enchanting music, faster and faster.

The parents stood like statues, unable to move. Then they began to shriek: "Oh, no! He's taking them to the river!"

However, at the river, the Piper turned, taking the path that led out of town.

By now, there were parents shouting outside the Mayor's house. "Do something! Pay the Pied Piper all he was promised and more," they begged. "Please don't let him take away our children."

"Don't worry! He can't take them far," the
Mayor answered, foolishly. "Our mountain
stands in his way, doesn't it? The children
can't climb those steep sides. They'll get tired
soon and come back. You'll see."

5

The Mayor's Lesson

How little the Mayor knew! The children
danced along the path, laughing and
singing until they reached the steep
mountainside. It seemed as if the Pied Piper
could lead the children no further.

Then he raised his arms and with a flash of light, a magic gateway opened in the solid rock. On went the Pied Piper, leading the children into the shining cavern beyond. Then, with an awful sound, the rocks closed up again. They were gone.

Only one poor child was left weeping
on the mountain. He could not hurry like
the others. "Oh, I will never reach that
wonderful land," the boy cried, bitterly.
"They will all be playing in the sunshine
and I will be here all alone."

The wretched Mayor wished he had kept his word, but it was all far too late. The children were gone forever. For years afterwards, every street in that town was silent and every home filled with sadness.

The parents searched all the valleys and mountains around and asked everywhere for their lost sons and daughters. However, neither the children nor the Pied Piper were ever seen again.

About the story

The story of *The Pied Piper of Hamelin* is a legend from the town of Hamelin in Germany. The earliest known record of this story comes from a stained glass window created for the church of Hamelin, which dated to 1284 CE. In 1384 CE, the town chronicles state "It is 100 years since our children left."

There are many theories about why the children left Hamelin. Some people think that the Pied Piper was a symbol of hope for a town dying of the plague spread by rats. Others think he was a symbol of death who carried off the children. He has even been seen as someone who sold the children into slavery or recruited them for a crusade.

Be in the story!

Imagine you are the Pied Piper and you are leading the children into the mountains. What do you want to say to the Mayor now?

Imagine you are the Mayor and the children have gone. What do you want to say to your townsfolk and to the Pied Piper?

Franklin Watts
First published in Great Britain in 2016 by The Watts Publishing Group

Text © Penny Dolan 2016
Illustrations © Martin Impey 2007

Series Editor: Jackie Hamley
Series Advisor: Catherine Glavina
Series Designer: Cathryn Gilbert

A CIP catalogue record for this book is available
from the British Library.

The artwork for this story first appeared in
Hopscotch Fairy Tales: The Pied Piper of Hamelin

ISBN 978 1 4451 4661 4 (hbk)
ISBN 978 1 4451 4662 1 (library ebook)
ISBN 978 1 4451 4663 8 (pbk)

Printed in China

Franklin Watts
An imprint of
Hachette Children's Group
Part of The Watts Publishing Group
Carmelite House
50 Victoria Embankment
London EC4Y 0DZ

An Hachette UK Company
www.hachette.co.uk

www.franklinwatts.co.uk

FSC
www.fsc.org
MIX
Paper from
responsible sources
FSC® C104740